BSF DIARIES

KRANTI

SUMEET KUMAR

Made with ♥ on the Notion Press Platform
www.notionpress.com

SUMEET KUMAR , A adult who experinces many phases of life , a well known writer and a writer of new era .In reality he is a writer as well as ,singer ,poeter ,shayr ,quote writer ,lyric writer and and a performer well as anchor or standup comedian.Very exicting and intresting fact about him is that he is author of new era i.e.

He starts his journey of writing at the age when he was going to schools to get the study .His streak of 200 books will be the great achievment for him in future ,His some famous works i.e Maturity of love (genre _Love) Privacy of dream (Genre -LIFE STYLE OF MIDDLE CLASS).

YOU CAN ALSO BUY MY BOOKS FROM NOTION PRESS ,ABE BOOKS ,IMUSIC IN ,FLIPKART ,AMAZON ,KINDLE ,INSTANT READ LIKE EBOOK ,KINDLE ,GOOGLE ,INTERNATIONAL SITES AND MANY MORE .

PODCASTER ON SPOTIFY :@BROKEN HEART

INSTA ID : BOOKHUB92

GMAIL: sumitkumar 88234

LINKEDIAN : SUMEET KUMAR

.

Contents

Contents

Preface

If there is anger instead of hard work in the dream, then leave them there because neither you will be able to be worthy of them nor they will be able to be for you.

This is not only the story of Anmol Rathore but of all those who work for four years but do not get jobs even after being qualified.

Engineering is a cursed in today's world, which neither we can remove from ourselves nor can we bring it closer,And that too because of those who do many promises at first, but when it comes to fulfill them, they become brokers of the seven.

Acknowledgements

SUMEET KUMAR , A adult who experinces many phases of life , a well known writer and a writer of new era .In reality he is a writer as well as ,singer ,poeter ,shayr ,quote writer

,lyric writer and and a performer well as anchor or standup comedian.Very exicting and intresting fact about him is that he is author of new era i.e.

He starts his journey of writing at the age when he was going to schools to get the study .His streak of 200 books will be the great achievment for him in future ,His some famous works i.e Maturity of love (genre _Love) Privacy of dream (Genre -LIFE STYLE OF MIDDLE CLASS).

YOU CAN ALSO BUY MY BOOKS FROM NOTION PRESS ,ABE BOOKS ,IMUSIC IN ,FLIPKART ,AMAZON ,KINDLE ,INSTANT READ LIKE EBOOK ,KINDLE ,GOOGLE ,INTERNATIONAL SITES AND MANY MORE .

PODCASTER ON SPOTIFY :@BROKEN HEART

INSTA ID : BOOKHUB92

GMAIL: sumitkumar 88234

LINKEDIAN : SUMEET KUMAR

.

CHAPTER ONE

UNEASE

The words I want to write today are very correct, because what I want to say are those things from the heart, which I always say to myself, because I do not want to understand the things of the world and the things of the society, but still there are some memories which I have left my mark like a house, I don't know what I want to become, I don't know what people have made of me, I just know that life is mine as it is, I am neither in this want to talk with someone or not I want to express it in front of someone because love is not the last pain that makes a person away from himself and there are many other things in this gathering that make a person weak, these words of mine are only with me. This is not happening, it is the safari of my soul which gives me as much special features of living even today as the memories, I always think that I wish I would leave this journey and go towards for other Destination but like never happened to me.

CHAPTER TWO

ETERNITY OF LIFE

Means life has become so merciless that sister-in-law asks for alms even to reach graveyard, I am that person, I have seen the same amount of happiness, instead of living I want to increase the fire, and I want to get away from all this. I am but there is no hope that I will be able to get away from them, I can never distance myself from them even after saying this, because this is my desire which if I pass through it once, I may fall in love with someone, now I am feeling scared. May I not get defeated by my own existence,

Because I decide the way but I am not able to decide life, every day when I cross that threshold to Gujarat, I feel that life is getting more and more from me, it is not even a matter that I do not have the desire to live, I want to open my sisters, wander in the streets and mountains, where even the wind is with me and only take the name of love and my paan, but nowadays dreams are fulfilled, if I say so, my wishes are unfulfilled. Will remain the same, this life will also be with us all the time ,Some roads are ours and some are strangers, I do not know whether I will fulfill my dreams or not, I do not know whether the brightness that I have shown in my wishes can fulfill my dreams. There is a feeling of living but it means that charity is not being known, what am I doing, what is my God in the world?

CHAPTER THREE

ELEVATED MEMORY

Will I ever recognize myself, I will burn that person's fire one day by making an identity of myself like the rest, I am not afraid of fire, nor did I hold back from sacrificing myself, yet I have a wish in my mind It remains incomplete all the time, and I cannot complete it even by saying it, I have to make every shadow of it equal within myself and build a wall of a new gathering on the foundation of my memories, which also ends in my name and in my name. finished but i don't know,When will I be able to do this, my feelings are now dominating me, I am not able to separate from myself even after saying this, I do not know what I want from me, but I know for sure that each and every wish of their limits is trying to distance himself from me.

CHAPTER FOUR

BELOVED

I have started talking since time immemorial, the closer I get to her, the more she loves me, but these days her desire has also faded like her friends whom she has never known, once they break up, there is no such thing that I can't go to that party again, I still have a lot of desire to go, but what crime has not been forgiven by my own court yet, what I think is that I don't know this all the time, that too from someone and so much, I wish I could I am such an innocent boy,Whose innocence is trying to be robbed in a gathering of some people, I can neither consider my own existence to be wrong, nor will I allow him to be wrong sometimes, but the question is still the same, have I really happened to him, what ever happened to me No, well, these words are about love, otherwise, sir, be careful with your words, because every small person who has eaten a small person, only the air of pain will be there, which will make them intoxicated and take them on such a path, which will be very difficult to handle.

CHAPTER FIVE

BROKE MY TIES

I end this journey but I don't want to leave it somewhere far away, I know that each and every memory of it will trouble me, and maybe it can destroy me as long as I have a gathering, but I myself don't know that God What is the pressure of pain, if its training was known even a little, then it would have removed it from its own mind long ago, but where is the hope? As long as I am maintaining a relationship, I am a human being, but the day I broke my ties with him, that day ,brutality may come to the fore, but on that day the training of my mother and father will be lost, the knowledge that they have given to me will be lost, well there are many moments, but there are some things that I am telling you in reverse, about bachelor life. I have ever heard, that means, until you express some pain, how will its path open, first of all, I have already included some words about it, that there is a little struggle, bachelor life is also very similar from one side

Like love, as long as it stays together, it keeps the desire to live alive, but the day its dead body is found in our dreams, that day life shows its true colors.

CHAPTER SIX

SEMI -LIFE

I don't know what I have lost in life, because today every safari of my past seems false to me, for which I used to die earlier, today life has become just like that pressure cooker, once it rings, it is felt that the journey continues. But if the same thing happens again, does it mean that we have decided on the path? Everything is not special to write because my story of public is also like that moon which does not have any light of its own.

Well, if the time is being lit, then it must be about that sun, because this story is also about the one who alone has always wanted victory in his life, no one loves the rays of the sun, And it is said that when you can walk without anyone, then on that day your life will become better and you will also go on a ride, why did you keep saying this, why have I ever felt these things, my life is just becoming barbola of all,In front, they say, if the relationship of pain is written in the pages, it means that life has shown many such conditions, seeing which I still consider myself weak. Earlier I thought that I have to go far away from everyone and now when I am away from them, It seems that why did I have to leave, that is why I had to leave that house, where even though my luck was not written in my favor, but there were things of peace, why did I leave that house where that every wall is filled with sweet memories.

CHAPTER SEVEN

DIE FOR RESPECT

I am still attached maybe , today in my own eyes I have lost even after winning Ayesha is feeling that why I got this life at all Nor does mother tell that love in her eyes, I never thought that I want to go away from my home, only her memories will become the support of living for me, do you all know that we are living in a brick house Why is it called a house, because its walls give us Keeps us safe from all that we are afraid of, that world is as good as it looks from outside, it is equally bad and dirty from inside, I don't know which way should I go? Because there are many ways but the destination is one, his dream is one and his hope is also one, I am that person whose happiness I want to swear now and the marriage procession too. People say that I am confused and maybe I also feel that I am confused, and God is confused that I do not see my dreams,Even though I have left my old city and its memories, but they will never leave me, what is a human being in the world? If he is rich then he gets peace and if he is poor then he gets bread for two times and if he is from middle class family then he earns respect and a pearl in exchange for which he can spend his future life well.

CHAPTER EIGHT

RETRIBUTION

I don't even know why I am writing this, but I can definitely feel that the things we do in emotion, I mean to say that when we try to break the wall of our patience and go ahead of it, they cross its limits. So life doesn't show anything to us, instead of childhood it makes our past even worse. If I say this to everyone, neither to live nor to die. Otherwise, will you be able to spend your whole life with him?

I don't think so because the way I have lived my life, even if I look at her from one side or the other, she is completely pale in comparison to my previous life and she is in love because earlier mother used to cook food with her hands. And today, when I prepare to eat Ushi with my own hands, there is neither affection nor any taste in it, after eating it, like feels great that she should never show her life to anyone on such a day, the lamp of the house came banging.

I don't think that the light that I left in that darkness every single evening will ever return to my eyes, but it's not that I'm not trying, but I'm going to think that what I eat How can I give the last impression of my future in that, the clear meaning of saying is that I have also made the relation of going away from my home, so if the tragedy of going to him is also from me, then maybe to this heart for a few moments, rightly so at ease ,well I had left every body of my home, now I need him because even if my grave is decorated, I want it to be decorated in that fire where every memory of my childhood was full of happiness and carefree. We see many things in life, but at that time we do not understand those faces because behind those faces, we can never remove them from ourselves, even if we lose our lives.

CHAPTER NINE

PHILOSOPHY OF PASSION

Life is also a book, whose receipt is a little silent on my side, I am aware of every pain in the world, which people call destruction and also in maybe . I am a journey among them, that God has given us life but he never taught us how to live Let's leave and we say go live your life if you can't walk according to us then you don't stay in our house could, he used to say these things for love because one of his also says that we should not repeat every little thing of our childhood in our youth, I have never lived like that. happiness is not only there, means there is soul inside the core of heart , but each and every body of it is always ready to take me away from itself, what did you teach? What Got training I don't know? I just know this much that today I am trying to write some words of everyone in the scale of my words, they say.

CHAPTER TEN

SCATTERED MEMORIES

UTTAR PRADESH

ADAUN ALIGARH

200201......

I have heard a lot about life, that too from childhood, people defame God too much that it is a game, otherwise it is a gamble, and more There are many things that are felt in his part but for me it is just a journey in which even today he does not want and he does not want love because?

Anmol Rathore

22\03\1998

ADAUN ALIGARH

Everything in the world is not written in destiny, in God's world whoever thinks that he is perfect means there are no mistakes in him. If something is not lacking, then that person is wrong, we are all scattered somewhere, some are scattered in someone's memories and some are in their dreams since childhood.

CHAPTER ELEVEN

CV

I was taught that if you want to live, then live with your hands closed, till today I could not understand that those who were good go away so soon, what about heaven? Vacancies are vacant in caste, so many good people go to work as employers, but when they go, why don't they come back? There are many questions in life since childhood, but if I started talking about them all, Can I write my incomplete story only? but still some questions,those who can stop the neighborhood of your heart on the right for a while, the first question is that till when will we be lost in the crowd of God and our own You will find every nook and cranny of existence, how long will you keep your CV like a lover even after studying for four years or taking a degree? In the name of the country's economy, we will increase our tax, till when will we students kill ourselves? So many things in the world, and this too in me ,

I also agree that on many problems it does not mean that there is no solution, today everything of the government seems to be false and that Ishqiye because they make promises every time but do not keep them, there can be a reason for that too, and that reason is that in whose teeth I am Once they shine, then they forget even their humanity, every thing of this countary has now been included in the art market, and we,

Why should we talk about things anyway, who breathes on their mother-in-law and who live their life like a human being in God's country. What about them?

CHAPTER TWELVE

HYPOCRITICAL WISH

Every single thought of theirs has become hypocritical today, and the sad thing is that we can say that they cannot get out of their place, hard work today only There is a word, not fire, earlier I also used to think that with my Mehta I would fulfill all my dreams which I used to see in my childhood but When the wind of luck struck them, they changed their ways, it is said that there are no winds in the nature of every human being, but the society is their own people.

When you try to lead them in that direction, at that time they cannot stop themselves to move away from that path, I have only heard that if someone If a person loses something that he loves very much and he cannot live with his veena, then his condition becomes exactly like that evening. time passes by showing its light, that too for humanity, I have also lost one thing, my life which was very important for me, but now it is mine.

I don't have it and I don't have anything special about living in maybe nowadays, but I didn't change at that time, I also thought what if he I don't care if I am not with you, I will try to get her back, but that wish never came true, but do all of you talk like me? What is that thing I am doing?

CHAPTER THIRTEEN

UTTAR PRADESH DIARIES

I have given this identity to Ishqiye above because I really needed it at one point of time, now everyone in Uttar Pradesh knows Anmol Rathore There is public, well behind this also there is a secret which you will definitely tell everyone, but first of all understand what we say, Bihar and Uttar Pradesh There is only one specialty that this kind of people come out, that too a crowd, one they can do anything for their mother earth and the other, those who feel good about themselves.

Can go to any extent to make it, this is a special thing about pistol, because even this some can be studied in school and pistol talk there is a lot, but it is not that there are no people studying in Uttar Pradesh, they are not capable, if they were not capable, they would have done for their mother earth. How is it included in the army in the row of lakhs? If it is good then it is also bad, but if the role of the scales of both is skewed then it is bad.

Always ahead that too well, and that love because it has also been started by some human being, life is playing a role in our life which Ordinary time and the destination of a person are very different, from childhood till today Baba has learned that if there is a nature to live life then love Stay away from him because he makes a person weak not strong, I don't know why he used to say these things to me, because there are other people in my house too.

CHAPTER FOURTEEN

THE ILLUSION KING

There were brothers and sisters to whom he could explain these things but he never revealed them in front of them, and on the other hand mother also taught me the same. Used to give from the date, that if you want to move forward, then learn to forgive people, you know that there is no bigger warrior than Lord Krishna in Mahabharata In that Kurukshetra, even then he did not raise his weapon to kill anyone, because he knew him only if he was of religion. If the protest goes on, then who will protect the religion?

I have grown up listening to these things since childhood, and one of its special things is that I can fight my battles from both sides, be it from the side of evil. From the good side, but this is not my story nor the beginning of my existence, I am saying these things out of love because any human being from childhood He does not become an animal, because this is illusion which is given to us by another person, and at that time we do not even understand the teachings given by him that,

Is it his wish to take us, well, I am going to take you all on a journey where nature can be written by my death? Wrote Ishlia because its bailout ever my life I am not only a little angel, that means the story is yet to be told, so why should we blind our eyes in search of its existence already?

CHAPTER FIFTEEN

PAVITRA SADAN

My dad who that he is a contractor by profession but till date he has never taken any contract, and my mother who is my whole world, she is a teacher by profession, Till now the whole house has been taken care of, so are my siblings, whose names are identified as Rohan, and Savi, Rohan who is my younger brother but the whole house.

Who is dear to us and the night of our small life, who is our friend, she is my mother's life, whose mother is never away from herself ,can't do anything else ,My only identity is that I am elder boy of Pavitra Sadan, Why is our house named Pavitra Sadan? because my mother's name is Pakhi Rathore and my father's name is Takshak Rathore, let me tell you one thing that our family is very complicated, means from childhood till today. Our life went on a flat track, whenever we see it, it keeps bouncing, and most of all it bounced when Corona's clock hit our country. I came to India, at that time there was such a shortage of money that the economy of our house went down completely, at that time I regretted for the first time that

Why did I become an engineer, because at that time I remember that it had been almost two years since I completed my degree and I still did not have a job, my mother He also told me that son, no matter how fearful you may be, but if your pocket is empty, then the world will also leave you among those people involved, whose dreams are big but he is not able to do anything special in his life, that day mother's words seemed true to me.

CHAPTER SIXTEEN

FOUR YEAR

Even did this, even went to people's doors for hours and hours to get a job, still I could not get a job, but got advice from many that you are like . If you didn't do it, your life would have been different today, I was shocked when I saw that boy who used to copy from me and somehow passed in the paper and on the other hand, who worked hard for four years, still till date I have nothing but four coins, that boy is now an assistant I have become an engineer and an assistant local, yes, but it is not that I do not have less, I have work, younger brothers and sisters go to school in the morning. Go to leave, then take food for father, then listen to mother's teeth at night and then go to sleep after eating food like shameless, four years passed like this. When someone went on vacation, corruption saw that he could not get a job because my mother was a teacher.

CHAPTER SEVENTEEN

22 February 2022

If I just erase my existence, maybe the problems of my house will be solved and their expenses too, and maybe I remember the day on which I decided I had done that enough is enough, now I have to leave this world, because only comedy was going on in life, I saw some like too. People give me sympathy and at least call me poor, that's why I thought on 22 February 2022 that it will go away soon, I mean to say That some end up dying by drowning in a deep river, because if like had done something by mistake at home, I would have died later but before that my This news first flourished in the locality, that too like Corona, I thought love jumps into a river, I can't even express it in my words. I was so broken that day when mother said that I wish I had only one girl in your place who would walk on my path and listen to me.

I would have done a job for money, but where have you obeyed me, you only obey your Baba, you have not done anything to him in your life. I had thought that you would do something, but you also turned out to be like them, there is a secret behind this as to why I had told these things to me, then the matter was something like this, That day Rohan was ill and Ma told me that I will not be able to return on time today, so you Carry Rohan and Savi to school and Rohan's health is very bad, so please suppress him and put him to sleep. I was very far away, my mother was an government teacher ,that's why Ma always used to come late, that's why Ma had already called me and told me to take care of son Rohan and till till I do not come, you will not move from the house, after all I listened to their words and then I also went Rohan and Savi school to carry them .

And as soon as I brought him with me, I took him with me and pressed Rohan as soon as he came. at that time everything was fine, but at the same time I got a call that Baba was also unwell, and this call What was done was that his laborers who loved him very much, even told him that we will leave him, son, you have come, but what should I do, my heart did not agree. After all, on whose shoulders the whole world had roamed in the meeting, how could he leave him alone in that condition, so at that very moment Rohan

Resolved and went straight to father and at that time father's health was also very bad. Before that I took him to Dr. Harish who is my father Brother-in-law seems to be from far away means my mother is also from far away, then as soon as I showed them and brought them home, it was 9 o'clock in the night. , That's why I went to Rohan and Savi's room first, but as soon as I went to their room, they didn't show me that, then I saw them ,I went to the terrace and saw him, but he was not there, after all, when he went, where did he go? I then also asked Kavita Aunty whether her Rohan and Savi have seen ?

CHAPTER EIGHTEEN

CONSTANT FIGHT

But I didn't say anything to him at the time, I didn't tell this thing to Baba because his condition was already bad, and if I would have called Ma So he got very scared, so after that he went straight to the next park which was almost a few blocks away from our house, but he was also not there , I was very scared at that time, and maybe cried for the first time in his life that day, before going to wash them somewhere else.

As soon as I got a call from my mother, I was afraid that what would she say to her that Rohan and Savi were not at home. But it was not even a matter of silence, because if anything had happened to her, Sayad would never have asked her to live after that. They say if time But in case of any shock, then human beings can try to return to their friends again and if at that time it is a little late than that. If he ignores, then it may also happen that his life may not be saved, I knew that I have lost something today, my mother's eyes, so I want to return her.

I will try too, but I realized for the first time on the same day that my fate is also written by Yamraj because neither two moments Couldn't live or kill, when mother's call came and when I went home to tell her Rohan, I am not getting Savi same as before I crossed the threshold of my house, at the same time my mother's sandal hit my face and as soon as it hit me, Rohan and Savi were also present in front of me.

what means?Is this a life, this is a game, I was not able to understand? Well that day Ma's beating didn't feel bad, it was her words which directly hit me. Where the mortal memories has joined, and on that time I cannot separate myself from myself even after saying that day, because whatever words he says to me on that day, his It was worth it too, because because of me someone's life could have been lost that day, and they say that deals are made for relationships, in the world of human life No, you all know whose deal I had made that day, my lonely brother, I was not even aware that this fanna was also written in my part, well Why do I say such a thing, let's go?

CHAPTER NINETEEN

LOVE SPECTACLE

Love is that spectacle in life which is not destined for everyone and those who have it never stay with each other till the end, in all the lives I have seen, I find myself in them all because there are people That I have only one of them in my life, and I have lost myself in them and I have lost myself in such a way that I do not even realize that my death has already reached my grave and I am lost in myself. begging to live, that day When Rohan was ill, I did not leave him, nor did I go to forget my happiness by ignoring him, I went to fulfill my duty which I have been trained since childhood and I could not forget him even after telling him. , I felt that all the happiness had happened that day in a jiffy, I could not understand what I was doing, I could even tell them the truth, but at that time I could not understand that I What should I say face to face?

On the one hand Baba's health deteriorated and on the other hand Rohan too, I thought as long as both of them were in sleep, I would take Baba with me, but fate had decided something for me that day, when I When I tried to say these things to him, he didn't even listen to me, then I want to tell him that I am not wrong, but before that both of them had met last, so Ma's pride: Ma I am telling the truth, I really have a It was important work, I had flown in love,And when I went out, I had suppressed Rohan and I had also put Savi to sleep.

CHAPTER TWENTY

PAINFULL CONVERSATION

"MOTHER: You don't even know what you have done for Anmol. If I don't come at the right time, then Rohan's life can also be lost today.

Anmol: What? (Astonished)

Anmol: Like what happened with Rohan that she could have lost her life, it was only a normal fever.

MOTHER: A normal fever, you don't even know Anmol that the daba you had given to Rohan was of expiry date, he had fainted after eating it, and if I had not come at the right time, today my Rohan would not be among us. Hota, how could you be so careless and what was the work that you left even your brother to die?

Invaluable : ....

MOTHER: Tell me Anmol, anyway you have completed your degree and you do not do anything, just sit at home all day long, he roams around with his loafer friends, you also know about Satish ji. The boy is worth lakhs today who is three years younger than you, I never expected you to turn out like your father, I am ashamed to call you my son, if you are your mother for your family And if you can't do anything for your brothers and sisters, then just do one thing and leave us alone...

Anmol: Why were there words of anger instead of concern for me in words?"

Lost In Silence

The silence had passed through and I was thinking at that time what have I lost? The one who beat me was only love for me, but after listening to those things, he never realized that when the moments of my Tabus have passed, I mean, I could not say anything to him, but am I right or not? Those who kept their words buried in their heart for a long time, finally spoke them in front of me, well, I was not bothered by their words too, but when their

Alphas I felt very much then maybe trouble had increased even more, I didn't say anything to him for a long time, just got out of Baba's bike and got ready to go on a journey, if I had gone in front of Ma, then maybe would not have let me go, that's why I went to my room first and then straight out the back door.

It was not that I was tired of listening to his words, but at that time I was feeling many things in which if I had said in front of him, Sayad would have lost his face, that day for the first time my Basanti was not with me, meaning I am settling my helmet, I cannot go far in love, otherwise the policemen catch me, and on the other hand, at that time the love of Corona was also less, but I knew where I had to go, which way that by training

To move towards my destination, I went towards the Yamuna Bridge in love, not to kill myself, but to be free for something, that too from the world which was my own but did not feel mine that day, of a very different kind. Thoughts were coming that day, some of those thoughts were such that I cannot even write in my words, someone said that if the path in life takes you somewhere, then stop for a while, better to go.

Vacant Luck

I wanted to stop myself at that time in love, the situation in the house had become such that I could not run away from him by saying that, before that, a different fan came in front of me towards my homes, that too Gross of the policemen, I don't know whether they were patrolling that too, I was sitting on the top of the bus bridge and they felt that I was going to commit suicide so they asked them first that after that they took my bike also sealed and after that did they leave me where I came from, that is, in my house, in the neighborhood thinking that I have done something wrong and at that time mother is thinking that she did something because of my speaking. , But before this they had some agreement, before that they all told that what else I was doing sitting on the bridge, what is the meaning? Life is neither giving a chance to die nor to live? Freedom from above had become a different fate in my life, I thought that They would be more worried about me if they would get some work in time, but unfortunately, they started drinking even more, and the people of the neighborhood who came to save me by saying that someone would have killed their elder boys like this. They also did not get children from my mother's hands at that time, they say that if rice is mixed with wheat, then pistachios are both at that time, but the one whose quantity is more, the stomach earns due to its effect. But heard from someone that there is no face of good times and bad,

Somebody wants to see the duration of time, I was tired that day of listening to mother's teeth and taking fake sympathy of the locality, I just wanted to get a job at that time, because now I can't stay in my house anymore, because its walls She was also asking me for employment, and I was really saying that I should get a job, and that day what I wanted happened, that means I really got a job, that too in the Border Security Force, they said that it was not vacant luck in hand.

Bsf

We should never worry about our luck, when I filled the BSF form, I didn't say anything that I wanted to join BSF, but when Santosh uncle was present with my offer letter That too in front of the whole locality, they say in pairs that Anmol has got a job, Anmol has got a job.

I will give, before that I will make a celebration. At last, the last wish of which I was eagerly waiting has been fulfilled, finally I got a job, but it was not just a job for me, it was my life, about which I never told my mother that I wanted to join BSF Because I thought that if there is a problem in dreaming, then first I should do all the hard work, I remained silent for that long in Ishqiye because I was waiting for the right time.

And at last that day has come, my life has come, that day even though people were dancing in the joy of getting my job in the whole locality, but there was someone who was still bereft of the sorrow of thinking of me, and that is none other than my family. Even today I cannot stop thinking about many things that he told me that day, but what were those things?

Edition 1

Some stories end before they even begin, but if their characters are alive, that means the story is still alive.

Printed by Libri Plureos GmbH in Hamburg,
Germany